4.2
2.0 pts.

GRANNY
TORRELLI
MAKES
SOUP

Also by
SHARON CREECH

Walk Two Moons
Absolutely Normal Chaos
Pleasing the Ghost
Chasing Redbird
Bloomability
The Wanderer
Love That Dog
Ruby Holler
Fishing in the Air
A Fine, Fine School

SHARON CREECH

GRANNY TORRELLI MAKES SOUP

DRAWINGS BY CHRIS RASCHKA

SCHOLASTIC INC.

New York Toronto London Auckland Sydney
Mexico City New Delhi Hong Kong Buenos Aires

ISBN 0-439-64875-0

12 11 10 9 8 7 6 5 4 3 2   4 5 6 7 8 9/0

Printed in the U.S.A.   23

First Scholastic printing, January 2004

Typography by Alicia Mikles.

For my granddaughter
Pearl Bella Benjamin

In memory of my grandmother
Marianna Fiorelli Licursi

and my mother
Anna Maria Licursi Creech

Contents

I. Soup

II. Pasta

1. Soup

That Bailey . . .

Bailey, that Bailey! He said to me, *Rosie, get over yourself!*

It was not a compliment.

I said, *Bailey, you get over your own self.*

Which shows you just how mad I was, to say such a dumb thing.

I'm Mad . . .

Bailey, who is usually so nice, Bailey, my neighbor, my friend, my buddy, my pal for my whole life, knowing me better than anybody, that Bailey, that Bailey I am so mad at right now, that Bailey, I hate him today.

Granny Torrelli Says ...

My granny Torrelli says when you are angry with someone, so angry you are thinking hateful things, so angry maybe you want to punch them, then you should think of the good things about them, and the nice things they've said, and why you liked them in the first place.

Granny Torrelli is always so reasonable, so calm, so patient, except maybe for the time a man tried to get into her house, pretending he was the meter reader, and she smashed the door on his foot and picked up a broom and opened the door again and beat him on the head with it and told him she had a gun (which she did not really have) and would use it if she had to.

Then she told him he was a pitiful excuse for a human being, going around like that trying to take advantage of old ladies (even though she normally does not like anyone else to call her an old lady).

Why I Liked Bailey . . .

Why I liked Bailey in the first place: Bailey was always there, born next door to me, one week after me, the two of us just two babies growing up side by side, our mothers together, and me and Bailey together, on the lawn, on the porch, on the floor, playing with pots and pans and mud and worms and snow and rain and puddles.

Help Bailey was what our mothers said to me. *Help him, will you, Rosie?* And I did. I always helped Bailey. He was my buddy, my pal, my friend. Went to the zoo, went to the park, had birthdays together.

What a smile that Bailey had! He was smiling mostly all the time, his hands waving out in front of him, sweeping the air. Freckles on his face, sticking-up hair very soft, very quiet Bailey boy, but not too quiet, and not pushy, not selfish, not mean, not usually.

I pretended he was my brother, only he was better than a brother because I chose him and he chose me.

So why does he go and be so spiteful? Why does he say *Rosie, get over yourself!* and why does he say that in that cold voice and slam the door in my face as if I am nobody?

Granny Torrelli Makes Soup . . .

Granny Torrelli comes over, says she's in charge of me tonight. She wants soup. *Zuppa!* she calls it. She says it like this: *ZOO-puh!*

She starts rooting in the refrigerator, selecting celery *(That's your green,* she says), carrots *(That's your orange,* she says), onions and mushrooms *(That's our white,* I say).

She reaches in the freezer, snatches some chicken, flips it into the microwave, zaps it to defrost. Seizes the big red pot, fills it with water, tosses in salt and pepper and a dash of soy sauce.

Hands me a knife. We chop, chop, chop, fling it all in the pot, such a good smell bubbling in the kitchen.

And then she says it: *Okay, Rosie, what's going on with you?*

I say, *Nothing's going on with me.*

She says, *You maybe can fool other people with that smart head of yours, but you can't fool Granny Torrelli.*

I love Granny Torrelli, always making good things, always so calm, so patient, always telling me about my smart head.

You Going to Tell Me?

Granny Torrelli roots in the cupboard, snares the little pasta dots, adds more pepper and salt to the bubbling good things, tosses in the pasta, and says, *You going to tell me what happened? You going to tell me what's making your eyes so inside-looking?*

She reaches out and taps underneath each of my eyes. It tickles.

Oh, it's nothing, I say. *It's just that Bailey.*

That Bailey? she says. *That Bailey? Your buddy, your pal—is there any other Bailey?*

I push my shoulders up, let them fall again.

Rosie, why are you so sad, inside-looking about Bailey? He is sick?

No, he is not sick, I say. *Except in the head, maybe.*

Granny Torrelli smacks her lips. *Rosie, that's no way to talk about your buddy, your pal Bailey.*

She frowns, a big clown frown, and pretends to sob. *Boo hoo hoo*, she says. *That Bailey has made me molto, molto sad. Boo hoo hoo.*

She makes me laugh, that Granny Torrelli.

Pardo . . .

Granny Torrelli hands me the wooden spoon. I stir the soup. It's smelling so good: all the green and orange and white swirling in the chickeny broth.

I am thinking maybe I will tell her about that Bailey, when Granny says, *I ever tell you about that Pardo?*

Pardo, I say. *Par-do.*

What? she says. *What's so funny?*

I never heard that funny name before.

Granny Torrelli puts her face up close to mine. She has little brown spots all over her face, bigger than Bailey's freckles. *Pardo?* she says. *That sounds funny to you?* She scrunches up her mouth, says the name again slowly. *Par-do. Par-do.* She grins. *Yes, I guess it does sound funny.*

But I will tell you, she says, *that Pardo was my buddy, my pal. We were like this*, she says, squeezing her thumb and forefinger tightly together. *We were inseparable, me and Pardo, Pardo and me. Skinny boy, black curly hair, enormous black eyes, and you know what? He had a smile, that Pardo, a smile just like Bailey's, that Bailey who is your buddy, your pal.*

And I loved Pardo, my granny Torrelli says. *I loved Pardo so much. I wanted to be with him every minute every day.*

Granny Torrelli sniffs the soup. *Stir*, she says. I stir.

What kind of salad? she says.

The one with oranges.

Eccola! she says, already rummaging in the refrigerator, gathering two oranges, some parsley, searching in the cupboard for the olive oil. She hands me a knife. We slice.

How come you didn't marry that Pardo? I ask.

Oh, you Rosie! she says.

No, really, I say. *Why didn't you marry that Pardo? How come you married Grandpa instead?*

Oh, you Rosie girl! We were just little, Pardo and me. Just kids. Bambini.

Like me and Bailey, I think. We are just kids. Twelve-year-old kids. *Bambini.*

Bambini...

We were little, me and Bailey, maybe three, maybe four, playing on the kitchen floor. Carmelita (his mother) and my mother were sitting at the table when Carmelita put her hands over her face and cried and cried.

When they went home, I asked my mother why Carmelita was crying so hard, so long. My mother pulled me onto her lap and said, *She is worried about Bailey.*

Why? I asked.

Because Bailey cannot see very well. Not like you and me.

She put a thin tissue over my face and turned me toward the light. *Like that*, she said. *See how cloudy everything looks? That's how Bailey sees.*

I could see blocks of white where the windows were and golden light from the lamps and the dark shadow of the stove. I turned my head this way and that.

That's why he falls, my mother said, *and bumps into things.*

I fall! I said. *I bump!*

She took the tissue from my face and kissed my nose. *Yes*, she said, *you fall and you bump.*

I took the tissue and climbed down from her lap and stumbled around the house with the tissue taped to my face, sweeping the air in front of me with my hands.

I must have taken that tissue to bed with me, because when I woke up the next morning, it was on my face. I felt it there before I opened my eyes, and in the dark behind my eyelids, I thought this: *At night Bailey and I see the same way.*

Just Like Bailey . . .

I wanted to be just like Bailey, and I wanted Bailey to be just like me. If he got green tennis shoes, I wanted green tennis shoes. If he could turn a somersault, I had to turn a somersault, too. If I had a cupcake, he had to have half. If I got new crayons, we had to get a second box for Bailey.

I do not even want to say what happened when I was supposed to go off to school the first day.

Un disastro! my mother said later.

As soon as my mother opened the front door that

morning, I dashed across the lawn to Bailey's house. *No, Rosie,* my mother said. *Bailey isn't coming with us.*

I keep going. Up the steps, pounding on the door. *Bailey, hurry up! Bailey, it's time for school!*

My mother coming up behind me and the door opening in front of me. Carmelita standing there, her lips pressed tightly together.

Get Bailey! I say. *It's time for school.*

Carmelita kneels in front of me. *Rosie, honey, Bailey has to go to a different school.*

No, no, no, no, no! I squeeze past her, run up the stairs. *Bailey, Bailey, Bailey!* I see him sitting on the floor of his room, fumbling with his shoelaces. *I'll help you, Bailey. It's time for school!*

Me, such a little girl acting like a mother.

I kneel down. Bailey puts his face right up against mine, so close our noses are touching. He smells like toothpaste.

Rosie, he says. *Rosie, can I come with you?*

Yes! I say.

Then my mother is there, lifting me up, and I am kicking and screaming, and she says, *Rosie, come with me. You'll see Bailey later.*

I still hear myself screaming for Bailey as my mother takes me outside and puts me in the car and fastens my seat belt and drives away, and I am screaming and crying and kicking the back of the seat, and then she pulls over by the park and gets out and takes me out of the car and carries me to the swings, where we sit for a long, long time.

And when we finally did go to my school, I wouldn't let go of her hand, and I wouldn't say my name, and I wouldn't sing the song, and I wouldn't play with the blocks or the little house, and I wouldn't drink the juice, and I wouldn't, wouldn't, wouldn't do any single thing because Bailey was not there.

Now I am twelve years old, and when I look back on that first day of school, I am sure the teacher thought I was a very, very disturbed child.

Put Your Feet Up . . .

The soup is almost done. Granny Torrelli sits down, props her feet up on a chair. *Come on*, she says, *sit yourself down. Put your feet up.* She always does this before we eat. She says people rush too much. She likes to take a few minutes to smell the food and relax before we go rushing around gobbling it up.

I wish your mom and pop were here to join us, she says.

They work too much, I say.

She lets a puffy sigh out of her mouth. *Everybody*

works too much, I know it, she says. *Work, work, work. Pay the bills. Work some more. You know why, don't you?*

Why they work? I say. *To pay the bills.*

Granny Torrelli crosses her arms over her chest. She is a roundish woman, soft and plump, but my mother—her daughter—is skinny. I am skinny, too. *They want a nice roof over your head, they want good food in your stomach, they want to get you shoes before the ones you have pinch your feet.*

She looks down at my feet. *Are those shoes pinching you?* she asks.

I wiggle my toes inside my shoes. I am tempted to say yes, but I don't. *No,* I say. *They're not pinching me.*

Granny wiggles her own feet. *Good. Now are you going to tell me about that Bailey?*

That's Granny Torrelli for you. She distracts you, gets you talking about your shoes, and then she asks the question that is really on her mind. I think I should study exactly how she does this. It could come in handy, that skill.

Oh, that Bailey! I say. *That Bailey is so full of himself!*

Bailey? she says. *You sure you mean Bailey, next-door Bailey, your buddy, your pal? Or are you talking about some other Bailey I don't know?*

I am wanting to tell her, but I don't know where to start. I want to tell it right, want her to be on my side, want her to agree with me.

You know how he has all that special stuff? I say.

Special stuff? What kind of special stuff?

You know, recorded books and Braille ones and—

Oh, she says, *that special stuff. Wait a minute. I've got to take a little pause—* And she gets up and goes to the bathroom.

While she is gone, I am thinking way back, about the time I was showing Bailey the alphabet and he kept holding the tablet right up to his nose, but still he couldn't see the letters, and I got the idea to use fat black markers to make the letters. I printed out BAILEY in tall fat black letters, and he held the tablet close to his face, and while he was saying *B-A-I*, his mother, Carmelita, came in the room and squeezed her hands on her worried cheeks and said, *Oh! Rosie! What a great idea!* and then Carmelita sat heavily on a chair and shook her head.

I should have thought of that, she said. *Why didn't I think of that?* And then she looked so sad that I felt as if maybe I'd done something wrong.

And I thought at the time that I could teach

Bailey everything I learned at school. But then, maybe it was the next year or the year after, Bailey got the Braille things. I couldn't make any sense of those dots. He tried to show me, but I couldn't do it, couldn't get it. He could read with his fingers. It seemed like a miracle what he was doing with those raised bumps on the page.

I told my mother we had to get the Braille things. *I'll check into it*, she said, but she forgot about it, and when I reminded her, she said, *Rosie, I'll check into it*, and time was going by, and Bailey was learning more and more, and I was feeling so left behind. And one day he was reading to me from the Braille book, his fingers moving so softly over the page, and I grabbed the book and ripped the page and then I told him it was an accident, that I hadn't meant to rip it.

But I *had* meant to rip it.

Plays . . .

We put on plays, Bailey and me, all the time, for as long as I can remember. When we were little, the plays were about a mother and a father and a baby (the baby was usually a stuffed animal), or a sister and a brother. We made up the stories as we went along. One day when we were doing one of the mother and father ones—maybe we were seven then—our lines went like this:

MOTHER (Rosie):   It's such a good day. Let's take the baby to the park.

FATHER (Bailey):   I don't want to.

MOTHER:	Yes, you do.
FATHER:	Did you hear me? I said I don't want to.
MOTHER:	Bailey, stop it, you're ruining the play.
FATHER:	I'm not Bailey. I'm the father, and the father doesn't want to go to the park.
MOTHER:	Why not?
FATHER:	Because I'm sick of all this responsibility!
MOTHER:	Bailey, cut it out.
FATHER:	I'm not Bailey. I'm the father.
MOTHER:	Well, cut it out, Father.
FATHER:	I don't have to cut it out if I don't want to. I'm leaving!

And with that, Bailey-Father threw the baby (my stuffed tiger) on the floor and left the room.

The next day Bailey came with a suitcase. He was going to stay with us a few days, my mother said. I was so happy! And I thought Bailey would be happy, too, but at night he cried, and I asked him if he was crying because he couldn't see, and he said, *No*, and he kept on crying, and I asked him if he was crying because he missed his mother, and he said, *No*, and I asked him if he was crying because he missed his father, and he said, *Yes, and he's never coming back!*

He hasn't gone anywhere, Bailey, I said. *You're the one who has gone away.*

But I was wrong. His father had gone away, and he didn't come back.

The Blind Woman . . .

Granny Torrelli comes back from the bathroom, sits back down, and says, *Now, where were we?*

Bailey, I say. *We were talking about that Bailey.*

Si, si, she says. *Bailey. And what were you thinking about while I was gone?*

I tell her about the plays, and then I remember another play, and I tell her about that one, too.

We were in the backyard, Bailey and me, when the idea popped into my head. *Let's do one with a blind woman and her husband,* I said.

Bailey waved a stick at me. *What are you talking about?* he said. *That's so stupid.*

Don't you say it's stupid, Bailey. Why is it stupid?

Bailey waved his stick in the air like a wand. *Blind woman? It should be blind* man.

Why? I said. *I can be the blind woman if I want to.*

Bailey threw his stick at my feet. *No, you can't,* he said. *You don't know the first thing about it.*

I was mad. *That's just stupid, Bailey, stupid, stupid, stupid. I can be whatever I want to be in our play, and if I want to be the blind woman, I can be the blind woman.*

Bailey turned and headed for the house. *Then go right ahead,* he said. *Be the blind woman all by your stupid self.*

That Bailey!

And so I did. I did a play all by my stupid self and I was a blind woman, but it is hard to be a blind woman all by yourself, with no one to talk to but your own stupid self. It doesn't make a very good play.

When I finish telling Granny Torrelli about the blind woman play, she smacks her lips that way she does. *Rosie, Rosie, Rosie*, she says. *You're a stubborn Rosie sometimes.*

Stubborn Streak...

You get that stubborn streak from me, Granny Torrelli says.

Yeah, sure, I say, thinking of my granny Torrelli, always so calm, so patient.

Listen, she says. *Let me tell you about stubborn me. Remember Pardo? Pardo with the name you think is so funny? Pardo found this dog, see? Big black mangy-looking dog slobbering all over the place. That dog was so big I thought it was a pony the first time I saw it.*

Pardo, he was going to teach that dog everything—

Sit! Heel! Come! Fetch! All day long he was outside with that big black dog. He named it Nero, which means black, which goes to show you that Pardo was not the most—how you say?—original boy.

So he is out there making poor Nero sit and heel and come and fetch and completely—completamente!—ignoring me. Me—his buddy, his pal forever! And I did not like it, not one piccolino bit!

I got it into my head that I would make that Nero—that big black mangy dog Nero—I would make him love me. I would make him love me so much that Nero would want to be with me all the time, and then Pardo would want to be with me all the time, too.

And so I ask Pardo if I can take Nero for a walk, and my plan is to take Nero to the woods and give him little chocolates, but Pardo says no, I can't take Nero because Nero is too big and will not obey me and I might get hurt.

And I am stubborn, Granny Torrelli says. *I am so stubborn like a donkey. I beg Pardo. I plead. I whine. And finally Pardo says, 'Bene!' He says I can go ahead and take Nero for a walk, and I know he has said this only to shut me up.*

And so I take Nero and set off across the fields. His leash is a rope and it feels good in my hand. And then Nero starts running, gallump, gallump, like a big huge horse thing, faster and faster, and the rope is pulling, and it is rubbing my hand raw, and I am yelling at Nero to stop, but he won't stop, and then I trip, and Nero is dragging me across the field and down a muddy bank and slosh *into the creek, when finally I let go and Nero races on, running to the woods.*

Granny Torrelli, sitting in our kitchen, looks at the palms of her hands as if she can still feel the rope burning.

What about Nero? I say. Did you find him?

Nero! Granny Torrelli says. *There I am all sore and muddy in the creek, and you are worried about that black mangy Nero?*

She makes me laugh, that Granny Torrelli.

That dog! she says. *I straggled through the woods all day long calling that black mangy dog, and when it is getting dark and I am cold and hungry and bruised and prickled, I go home. I am not wanting to face Pardo. I am not wanting to tell him I have lost his most precious dog.*

I start back across the fields, and there are Mama and Papa and my brothers and sisters, and there is Pardo, and they are all coming across the fields like a big wave of people, calling for me, and I want to cry, it is such a good sight to see, but then I see Nero loping along beside Pardo, just as happy as can be, that black mangy dog!

And everyone is saying, 'Where were you?' and 'Blessed Mother Mary, you are safe!' but I am only seeing that black mangy Nero slobbering beside Pardo, and I go up to Pardo and I punch him and tell him he has a stupid, stupid dog. Stupido!

Granny Torrelli finishes her story and leans forward, placing both her hands flat on the table. *See?* she says. *See how stubborn I can be?*

And we laugh, me and Granny Torrelli, there in the kitchen with the chickeny soup smelling so good.

Tutto Va Bene . . .

Granny Torrelli stirs the soup, takes a big sniff and says, *Tutto va bene!* She says it like this: *Too-toe vah BAY-nay!* It means 'all is well.'

I am thinking about Granny Torrelli and Pardo and the black mangy dog, and that reminds me of the dog *disastro* last year. And while Granny Torrelli is dipping the ladle into the soup and pouring the soup into the bowls, she is reading my mind. She says, *Rosie, are you still wanting a dog for Bailey?*

I say, *That Bailey! He can get his own dog!*

Granny Torrelli says, *Puh! You're such a sassy Rosie girl today.*

And so I am thinking about the dog *disastro* as Granny ladles out the steaming soup. It started at school last year. A man came to assembly with his guide dog, a beautiful sleek golden dog. And the man showed us how his dog was his eyes and how it helped him get around the city and his house, and he said that even if he got lost all he had to say to his dog was: *Find home!* and the dog would lead him home.

It seemed like a miracle! I wanted one of those dogs for Bailey! I went rushing home after school and racing up the steps to Bailey's house and banging through the front door like a blast of wind, and I found Bailey in the kitchen, and I said, *Bailey! Bailey! You need a guide dog! They're the most amazing things! You'll never be lost! You'll never bump into things! You'll never—*

And Bailey said, as cool as can be, *Rosie, I know about guide dogs.*

What? I said. *What do you know about guide dogs? You never told me anything about guide dogs.*

And Bailey, sitting at the kitchen table, crossed his arms and leaned back in his chair and said— not in a mean way, but in a kidding way—*Rosie, do I have to tell you EVERYthing?*

And I said, *Yes, Bailey, yes, you do. Now what about it? Let's get you a guide dog!*

Can't, he said. *You have to be sixteen.*

What? I said. *Well, that's just stupid. Sixteen? Lots of kids have dogs, lots of kids who aren't sixteen.*

Not guide dogs, Bailey said. *You have to know a lot of special things. You have to train. You have to—*

Blah, blah, blah. On he went with the rules about guide dogs.

When I left Bailey's, I went out looking for a dog. I had seen a stray mutt hanging around the delicatessen, and I went in search of it. No luck. Next day, looked again. No luck.

Next day, looked again. Found him! Shaggy little brown-and-white, funny-looking dog. I petted him. Cuddled him. Lured him home. Snuck him into the garage. Brought him meat loaf, mashed potatoes, and gravy leftovers.

Wanted to do everything in one day. Sit! Heel! Stay! Mutt would not listen.

Locked him in the garage. Snuck out in the morning and fed him more meat loaf. Took him out to do his business. Made him a bed out of my pillow and an old blanket.

Went to school.

Came home. Pillow in a thousand, thousand shreds. Blanket peed on. Poop by the lawn mower.

Took him out. Sit! Heel! Stay!

Dog doesn't listen. He runs, rolls, bites my shoelaces.

Another week of that. Garage looking very bad, smelling very bad. Mom starting to ask about disappearing leftovers.

Little boy and his mother come to our door one day, asking about a dog. *Tootie is his name*, they say. Tootie! It's the little boy's dog, and he lost it and he is sad. They say someone down the street said they saw me with a dog that looked like Tootie.

My mother says, *Rosie doesn't have a dog, honey.
We're so sorry.*

They start to go. Hear barking. *Tootie!* the boy
says. His whole face lights up, as if someone has
given him a barrel of chocolate.

Boy and his mother head for garage. My mother
follows. I creep behind. My mother opens the
garage.

Tootie! the boy says, and that Tootie mutt runs
smack into the boy and licks him all over, and my
mother is looking around the garage and gagging
from the smell, and she says, *Rosie? Do you know
anything about this?*

Tutto NON va bene. All is NOT well.

And that was the end of the secret guide dog
business.

Pasta Party...

Zuppa is on the table!

Granny Torrelli folds her hands and says a little prayer. *God bless Mama and Papa and Rosie and Angela and Carmen and Giovanna and Lucia and Maddalena and Gianni and Lorenzo and Guido—*

On she goes like that, more and more names, and when she finishes, I say, *Ditto. I don't know who all those people are, but ditto.*

Granny Torrelli, with her hands still clasped together, says, *Oh, Rosie! You know! Giovanna and*

Lucia and Maddalena—those are my sisters—and Gianni and Lorenzo and Guido—those are my brothers, may they all rest in peace.

Oh! I say. *Are they all dead? All of them?*

Granny Torrelli says, *Puh! I do not like that word 'dead.' They are all having a big pasta party up there*—she lifts her palm toward the ceiling—*just waiting for me, the baby!*

Well, don't you go being in any big hurry to join their party, I say.

Puh! Granny Torrelli says. *I'm not going anywhere. I'm staying right here with my Rosie.*

And we eat our *zuppa,* and I am thinking about how Granny Torrelli left Italy when she was sixteen and she came on a boat with her uncle to America. And she has told me this before, but I ask her anyway, *And did you never see your family again, not ever?*

Granny Torrelli slurps her *zuppa*. She shakes her head. *Not ever.* Then she crosses herself because she is Catholic, but I am not Catholic and so I do not cross myself.

I can hardly stand the thought that Granny Torrelli never saw her family again, not ever, and that now they are all—her mama and papa and sisters and brothers—all of them are up in heaven having their pasta party, and my grandpa Torrelli is probably with them, and here is Granny Torrelli with just me, sipping chicken *zuppa*.

Tangled Head . . .

It's good zuppa, I say.

Granny Torrelli nods her head and says, *Si, si. We did good.*

You really think your mama and papa and brothers and sisters and Grandpa Torrelli are all up there—I raise my hand to the ceiling like Granny Torrelli did—*having a pasta party? And is Pardo there, too?*

Granny Torrelli puts one hand to her lips. *Pardo? Oh, Rosie, you don't want to know about it.*

I do!

Oh, Rosie, Rosie, Rosie. I will tell you later.

Is it sad? I ask.

Granny Torrelli places her hand over her heart.
*Si, Rosie, si. Molto, molto sad. You do not need all
those sad things in your smart head.*

I wish I had all the things in Granny Torrelli's
head inside my head, and then maybe I would
know what is going to happen to me, and who I
will be, and what I will be, and if I will marry, and
if I will have children, and if I will have a job,
and if I will be happy in my life.

What I say to Granny Torrelli is only part of that:
I wish I had the things in your head inside my head.

*Oh, Rosie! I wish I had a young head like yours,
instead of this old head of mine. You should not wish*

for all these tangled things in my head. She taps her forehead. *Very crowded in here!*

She passes me the bread. *Now,* she says, *let's get back to that Bailey.*

There she goes again.

Lost . . .

I glance out the kitchen window toward Bailey's house next door, but I can see only the front yard and the bushes hugging the house. A piece of red paper skips over the grass, doing flips in the breeze, and I think of Bailey when he was little and had a red sweater.

One day Carmelita came running to our door. *Bailey is missing! Bailey is gone!* And my mother and I rushed with Carmelita up and down the street and around the block calling, *Bailey! Bailey! Bailey!* and we stopped everyone and asked if they had seen Bailey, dressed in a red sweater and blue shorts.

And people joined us, all the neighbors, old and young, racing up and down the streets shouting, *Bailey! Bailey! Bailey!*

And someone called the police, and now the police were roaming up and down the streets asking people if they'd seen Bailey in his red sweater and blue shorts.

Bailey was never supposed to go anywhere alone, never, never, never.

Carmelita was out of her mind with worry. *He's been kidnapped! Who would do such a thing? Oh, Bailey, Bailey, Bailey!*

And when it started to get dark, we went home to get flashlights, and there was Bailey sitting on his front porch in his red sweater and his blue shorts, eating a peanut butter and jelly sandwich.

And maybe it was like when Granny Torrelli lost

Nero, Pardo's black mangy dog—maybe we looked like a big wave of people coming down the street and all of us saying, *Bailey! Bailey! Bailey! Oh, Bailey, you are safe!*

But Carmelita did not punch him, and she did not call him *stupido* like Granny Torrelli called Nero. Carmelita wrapped her arms around him and kissed him all over his face and cried and cried and cried.

The police came again, all of them smiling, so happy to see the red-sweatered boy with his mother. One of them said, *Where were you, Bailey?*

And Bailey untangled himself from his mother and brushed some bread crumbs from his red sweater and he said, *I went for a short walk that got very long.*

You were lost! I said.

Was not! he said.

You were!

I wasn't! Maybe you were lost, Rosie, but I was not lost! I wasn't!

And Bailey, my buddy, my pal, punched me and ran inside the house.

Now *that* was like Granny Torrelli.

I was mad at Bailey. I ran across the yards, up my steps, into the house, up more steps, and into my room, slammed the door, dove into the bed, pulled the covers up right over my head, and I was thinking I would sob, but instead a big smile appeared on my face.

I felt very happy that none of the horrible things I had been thinking as we ran up and down the streets—none of those awful, horrible, ghastly

things I feared might have happened to Bailey—
none of those things happened. None of them.

He only took a short walk that got very long.

The Prince...

Granny Torrelli sits up straight, bangs her spoon on the table, and says, *More zuppa! I want zuppa!*

I get up. *Yes, madam queen,* I say as I refill her bowl.

And then I tell her about the time that I was coming home from school—maybe I was ten then— and two older girls followed me: nasty, mean girls looking for a fight. I walked faster and faster and had just turned the corner of our street when they started pulling at my hair and grabbing at my books and telling me I was a stupid skinny girl, and I told them to cut it out. *Stop it, stop it, stop it!*

But they were pushing and slapping and whacking me on the head with my books, and I was trying to get away when all of a sudden, there comes Bailey running up the street.

I'd never seen him run so fast. I was afraid he would fall. How did he know nothing was in his way? How could he run so straight? How did he know I was in trouble?

Bailey is tall for his age and strong, and I was so glad to see him coming, but I was afraid, too—afraid that the girls would hurt him, would take advantage of his not being able to see.

Bailey said to the girls, *Hey, cut it out!* He was wearing sunglasses, something new he'd started doing so people wouldn't stare at his eyes.

The girls blinked at Bailey, standing there so tall and strong, and they stopped pushing and whacking me and backed away.

They don't know, I thought. *They don't know that Bailey can hardly see.*

Come on, Rosie, Bailey said, and I gathered up my books, and we walked on down the street, just like that.

Bailey, I said, *how did you know I was there? How did you know I needed help?*

And then he bowed low and said, *I hear really, really good. And I am your prince—Prince Bailey—and I came to your rescue.*

That Bailey!

The Rescuer . . .

We finish our *zuppa*, and Granny Torrelli places the sliced oranges on two salad plates, and then she sprinkles olive oil and salt and pepper and parsley over the top.

Isn't that something? she says. *That Prince Bailey coming to your rescue!*

Yes, I say, *it was something.*

And I am thinking how *I* want to be the rescuer. I want to rescue Bailey. I want to fix him, give him new eyes, make everything easier for him.

And Granny Torrelli, that mind reader, she knows I am thinking about Bailey, and she says, *So, Rosie, are you going to tell me about that Bailey? Why you are so mad at him today?*

I get up, go get the Braille books, bring them back to the table. *Watch*, I say.

And I open a book and close my eyes and run my fingers over the raised bumps and I read. I am still a little slow, but *I read!* And when I stop and open my eyes, Granny Torrelli is sitting there with her eyes sparkly shiny wet.

Oh, Rosie! she says. *You did it! That smart head of yours! It is like a miracle! Show me!*

And so I kneel beside her, and I put her fingers on the page and let her feel the bumps which are letters and words. *It's hard*, I say. *You need to start with just a few letters.*

She hands the book back to me. *It's a miracle, Rosie. Bailey must be so proud!*

I close the book. *No,* I say. *Bailey is not proud. Bailey is mad. That Bailey boy!*

And so I tell her what I have been wanting to tell her all night—about how it took me a whole year to learn the Braille, in secret from one of my teachers at lunch every day, sneaking the books home, opening them at night in bed, wanting it to be a surprise to everyone, but especially, most especially, to Bailey.

And today after school I went over to Bailey's, so excited to show him. I flopped on the couch, yakking away about this and that, and casually—oh so casually—I reached for one of his Braille books and I opened it.

He was sitting on the floor, his back against my knees. He heard the book open. *What book is that?* he said.

I told him.

One of mine? he said.

Yes, I said. *Want me to read you a little bit?*

He laughed. *Sure*, he said, *sure, you just go right ahead and read!*

He was feeling very smug, I could tell, so sure that I couldn't read his Braille book.

I let my fingers move across the first line, and then I backed up and started at the beginning, reading aloud: *There is a place where I often go. It is cool and calm—*

Bailey whipped around, put his hands out, found my hands on the book. He pushed my hands away and grabbed the book and ran his fingers over the page rapidly.

You cheated, he said. *You probably got the regular book and memorized the opening.* He slammed the book shut.

I grabbed the book from him. *I didn't cheat, Bailey. Listen.* I opened the book again and read the whole first page, and as I was reading it got very quiet, as if Bailey were not even breathing, and when I finished I felt so proud, and I thought Bailey would be so happy, so proud. I looked up at Bailey, but Bailey was not happy, was not proud.

He said, *You think you're pretty smart, don't you, Rosie?*

Yes, I said.

Well, get over yourself, Rosie!

What?

I said, 'Get over yourself, Rosie!'

I felt as if all the blood in my body were pouring down, down, down right out the bottom of my feet. I got up, started for the door, expecting, hoping, wishing he would stop me, but he didn't stop me.

I opened the door, stepped out onto the porch, with no words in me, no breath in me, just a loud wail going on in my head and *slam*!

Just like that, Bailey slammed the door behind me as if I were nobody, no buddy, no pal, just a nuisance nobody.

Why, Why, Why?

Oh, Rosie! Granny Torrelli says.

Why? I ask her. *Why did Bailey say that mean thing to me and slam the door on me? Why?*

Granny Torrelli presses her knuckles to her cheeks and says, *Hmmmmm. This is a tough one, Rosie.*

And then Granny Torrelli does a strange thing. She opens her hands and places them over her eyes, and I hear a little sound and see her chest moving up and down, and I can hardly bear it. Granny Torrelli is crying.

And I get up and stand behind her, patting the top of her head, and I say, *Don't cry, please don't cry!* And I am feeling so miserable because I have made two people unhappy today, and I don't even know why or how.

Granny Torrelli wipes her eyes and motions me to sit beside her.

What did I say? I ask.

Oh, Rosie, Rosie, Rosie. You and Bailey, you are like me and Pardo, and you made me think about him.

And so she tells me about the last day she saw Pardo. They were sixteen. She was going to America in a few days with her uncle. Pardo begged her not to go, but she wanted to go. America was everything! It sounded dazzling to her, full of everything, full of promise and excitement.

She wanted Pardo to come, too. Her uncle would

loan him the money for the boat fare. But Pardo said it was crazy. She should stay in Italy with her family, with him, and they would get married, and they would have children, and he would work, and she would raise the children and cook and clean and be the mama.

And my granny Torrelli told him she didn't want to cook and clean and be the mama. She wanted to go to America and have adventures.

Pardo got mad at her and told her she was too full of herself, full of impossible dreams, full of crazy wishes. He told her, *Go then! Go!*

And she was so angry with Pardo and went home that night and packed her one suitcase and did not leave her room until the day came when her uncle took her to America.

And Pardo never wrote to her and she never wrote to Pardo, and one day she got a letter from her sister saying that Pardo was untangling his black mangy dog Nero from the train tracks where his rope leash was stuck, and the train came and . . . and . . . that was the end of Pardo. He was squished.

And so, Rosie, every day I am sorry I was so mad at Pardo, sorry I didn't write to him, sorry he did not know how much I loved him.

And we sit there. Quiet. Granny is thinking about Pardo, and I am thinking about Bailey, and we are not eating our salad of oranges.

In My Head . . .

I am thinking about Bailey and Pardo. I am wondering why Granny Torrelli didn't stay in Italy, but then she wouldn't have married my grandpa Torrelli, and she wouldn't have had my mother, and my mother wouldn't have had me—not this me.

And I am wondering why Granny Torrelli never wrote to Pardo, and why Pardo never wrote to her, and why that still bothers Granny Torrelli now, after all these years.

And she gives me an answer out of the air, as if she knows my question. She says, *Rosie, I was such a stubborn girl! Too stubborn to write a letter. Too stubborn to say sorry. And here is the thing I learned: A friend like Pardo does not come along every day.* She pokes at her oranges, shiny with olive oil sprinkles.

And then out of the air I sense something about Bailey and the Braille books. Until today, Bailey could do something that I could not, and he wanted that and needed that.

It hits me *zap!* Just like that.

Granny Torrelli, I say. *Let's go to Bailey's. Let's take some zuppa to Bailey and Carmelita.*

Granny Torrelli hops out of her chair. *Si, si, si!* she says. *Zuppa for Bailey and Carmelita!*

She pulls out a plastic bowl, pours in some soup. *Bread, too*, she says, grabbing the loaf.

Oranges? I say.

Si, si, si! Oranges for Bailey and Carmelita!

We zip around the kitchen, dash out the door with our *zuppa* and bread and oranges, and we slip across the lawn and up the steps and knock on the door, and suddenly my heart is thumping like a little frog in my chest because what if Bailey slams the door again, and what if Bailey is still mad, and what if Bailey doesn't want our *zuppa* and bread and oranges?

The Door Opens...

Carmelita opens the door, a big smile on her face when she sees Granny Torrelli. They hug and start chattering in Italian.

Carmelita waves her hand toward the stairs. *Bailey's up there*, she says. *Go on.*

She doesn't know about our fight, I think. I go up the stairs slowly, afraid. I do not want another door slammed in my face.

Bailey must hear me coming because he stands in his doorway looking toward me.

Bailey! I say. *Don't you be mad at me. I am a stubborn Rosie, and I am full of myself, but I don't want you to be mad at me. And I will stop reading Braille and—*

Wait, he says, and he goes back into his room and returns with a blank piece of paper, which he hands to me.

What? I say. I am thinking he is being mean, playing a mean joke, giving me a blank piece of paper, but then I look closer, and there are little bumps on it, and I run my fingers across it. There are just two words to read, and those two words are *I'm sorry*.

And I hug Bailey. I hug the living daylights out of that Bailey boy!

And we do not talk about it, not this day. Instead we go downstairs, and we sit at the table, me and Bailey and Granny Torrelli and Carmelita, and we eat more *zuppa*.

Tutto . . .

In the dark, Granny Torrelli and I slip back across the lawn with our empty bowls.

Very, very good zuppa, I say.

Si, si, si, Granny Torrelli says. She glances back at Bailey's house and then at me. *Tutto va bene, Rosie.*

All is well.

That *zuppa*, that Granny Torrelli, that Bailey boy!

II. Pasta

She's Back...

Granny Torrelli is back. It's Saturday, Mom and Pop are at work, and Granny Torrelli is in charge.

We're making pasta! she says as she breezes in the door and sheds her coat. She rubs her hands together. *Pasta, yum!* She squeezes my cheeks with her soft fingers. *How's my Rosie girl today?*

Good, I say.

Bene! Now go get that Bailey. We need his help.

I dash out the door, race across the lawn, and up

the steps, fling myself into Bailey's house, calling, *Bailey, Bailey, Bailey boy! Wanna make pasta with Granny Torrelli?*

Bailey stands at the top of the stairs, tall and strong, his soft hair catching the light from the window on the landing. He smiles that great Bailey smile.

Sure, he says, and he is already feeling his way down the stairs, calling to his mother, *Going to Rosie's, Ma.*

I hear her call, *Okay, Bailey. Hi, Rosie, 'bye, Rosie!*

I am a little shy with my buddy, my pal Bailey today. We are over our fight about my being too full of myself. That's over and done! But there's something else squeezing in between us, something new, something I don't like, not one *piccolino* bit. And Bailey doesn't even know it, not yet. That Bailey boy. What am I going to do with that Bailey boy?

Ciao . . .

Ciao, Bailey, Granny Torrelli calls out as we come in the door. She says it like this: *Chow*. It means both 'hi' and 'good-bye.' I like that little word *ciao*.

Ciao, Granny Torrelli, Bailey says. He moves up close to her and lets her kiss both his cheeks, that way she does.

She's already got the big wooden pastry boards on the table and the bowls on the counter, and she is plucking things from the cupboard and refrigerator: flour, salt, eggs. *Aprons*, she says, *we need our aprons!*

I find the big white aprons in the closet and slip one over Bailey's soft hair and tie it for him. Granny Torrelli snares the wooden spoons and looks around, checking to see if she's got everything she needs. *We are going to make some superior pasta today*, she says.

Bailey smiles. He loves Granny Torrelli.

Granny Torrelli pushes a bowl in front of Bailey and takes his hand to show him where the bowl is. Then she hands him the bag of flour. *Go ahead*, she says, *dump some in. I'll tell you when to stop.*

Flour dust sifts into the air.

You two wash your hands, she commands. We obey.

She hands me the salt. *Four pinches*, she says. This is how Granny Torrelli measures, in pinches.

Big pinches or little ones? I ask.

Medium, she says.

I squeeze out four medium pinches of salt, and then I start to reach for the eggs, but Granny Torrelli touches my hand lightly, stopping me. She puts Bailey's hand on the eggs. Then she moves his hand to another empty bowl. *Crack them into that bowl*, she says to him.

That Granny Torrelli. Me, I always want to do things for Bailey because he can't see, things I think are too hard for him, like cracking the eggs. But Granny Torrelli is showing me that Bailey doesn't need so much help, that I should quit being such a take-charge Rosie.

Rosie will pick out the shell bits, she says, and I do.

It is good being in the kitchen with Granny Torrelli and my buddy Bailey, and I want to slow the day down so I can keep Bailey here with me all to myself.

My Warm and Cold Heart . . .

Bailey is whisking the eggs with a fork, all that gooey yellow swirling around, and I am watching his hands, and my heart is so full of that Bailey boy that I want to grab him and hug him. But I don't.

Instead, I can't help it, I think about that Janine girl, that new girl up the street, that too-friendly new girl, and just like that, my heart switches from warm to cold. I am ice girl, ice queen. That Janine girl, she is making my mind swirl.

First day she moves in, I go over and introduce my Rosie self. She smiles all over the place, especially when she finds out we are the same age and will go to the same school. She tells me I can help her find her way around, that she is so glad, so very, very, very glad to know someone in her new neighborhood so soon! Isn't she so, so, so lucky? she asks me.

She is a pretty girl, I give her that, with cool frizzy black hair, and she is so confident, that Janine, flipping her head this way and that, flashing her sparkly white smile, no braces or anything.

Do you have a best friend? she asks me.

Yes, I say.

She puckers her pretty mouth. *Oh, crud! I left my best friend in New York. I was hoping you could be my new best friend.*

I am thinking, *Hold on a minute. You don't even*

know me and I don't know you. It takes a while to be best friends. But I don't say that. Instead I say, *My best friend is Bailey. That's a boy. I don't have a girl best friend.*

I am surprised I say this because I do have a girl best friend, and that is Marlee at school, but Marlee is not allowed to go anywhere except school, and I am not allowed to go to her house because her father is very creepy, and maybe I am thinking I could use a second-best girl friend.

Janine says, *A boy for your best friend? How strange!*

I am about to tell her there's nothing strange about it at all, when she says, *That doesn't count, a boy being your best friend, so I'll be your best girl friend.*

I make my mouth smile. Part of me is very suspicious of this Janine girl. I don't want an instant best friend. But part of me is flattered that she must like what she sees of my Rosie self, to want to be my friend so fast.

I am thinking all this as Granny Torrelli makes a well in the flour and pours the gooey yellow egg glop in the middle. She says, *Okay, the fun part now. You can squish it all together. Take turns.*

And so Bailey and I take turns squishing the flour and eggs with our hands, and we are laughing and making a mess, and my heart is warm again, just like that. I am an odd Rosie girl.

What's New?

Bailey and I are taking turns mooshing the flour and egg goo, and our hands are sticky. Granny Torrelli sits down and props her feet on a chair and says, *Okay, so what's new here on Pickleberry Street?* She's such a goof. Our street is Pickburr, but Granny always calls it Pickleberry.

Nothing much, I say.

Oh, really? Granny says. *A whole week goes by since I've been here and nothing happened? Niente? Zero?*

Bailey laughs. *Well,* he says, *that new girl moved in.*

I am instant ice queen.

What new girl? Granny Torrelli says. *You mean a brand-new girl, like a baby girl? Or you mean a girl who is new to Pickleberry Street?*

I say nothing. My tongue is frozen. My lips are ice.

Bailey says, *Tell her, Rosie. Tell her about Janine.*

My eyes are freezing solid, round ice globs. My ice words drip out: *You tell her, Bailey.*

Granny Torrelli gives me a look. I know that look. It means, *What's up with you, Rosie girl?* I smoosh my hands in the dough, study the sticky mess, say nothing.

Bailey doesn't hear my ice, or if he does, he pays no attention. His sticky hands are suspended in the air while I am having my turn at the dough.

His head is tilted up slightly as he responds to Granny Torrelli.

Janine moved into the old Wicker house, you know which one?

The yellow one across from you? Granny asks.

No, the green one, Bailey says. *Yellow one's still empty. The new girl is the same age as me and Rosie. Really nice girl, isn't she, Rosie?*

I am mangling the almost-dough, strangling it. *Mmph* is my reply.

What? Bailey says, hearing my snotty voice. *You like her, don't you?*

Granny is giving me the look, big time. I stop being a jerk, temporarily, and say, *Sure, she's nice.* But my snotty self has to add, *I guess.*

Bailey turns his head toward me and my tight, stingy voice, and he says to Granny, *Well, she seems nice to* me. *Funny girl, too, always laughing, and very curious, wants to know why and how and all that.*

My ice queen has turned into a tiger, rumbling in me, wanting to pounce on that Bailey boy. I am thinking, *I am nice, I am funny, I am curious!*

Granny Torrelli, the mind reader, says, *Sounds like my Rosie girl. So maybe you and Janine will be friends, Rosie?*

I am too busy strangling the dough to answer. I am thinking how that Janine girl made me introduce her to Bailey, and how she swooned all over him, wasting her smiles and tossing her head at someone who couldn't even see her. And when she figured *that* out, she cooed and patted him, like he was a little dove, and Bailey smiled his big smile at her, and I wanted to throttle them both.

I am wanting to push Bailey out of the house and tell Granny Torrelli all this so she will be on my side and know why I am being an ice-queen-tiger Rosie, when Bailey says, *Janine is dying to learn Braille.*

Whaaaat? I say. I think my tiger is going to leap out of me, chew Bailey alive.

Don't sound so surprised, Rosie, Bailey says. You *wanted to learn it, didn't you?*

My words are so tangled in my head, I don't know where to start. Little mutters come out of my mouth. *Buh-uh-muh—*

Then Bailey says the worst thing: *So I'm going to teach her.*

Even Granny Torrelli knows why this would make me crazy. She knows how hard I learned in secret, how long it took me, and how Bailey was mad at me at first. She knows my head must be crazy with wondering why he would so quickly offer to teach Janine, when he never offered to teach me.

Bailey must sense something in my mutters, because he says, defensively, *Well, she asked me. Begged me! What was I supposed to say?*

That Bailey boy. I am wanting to take this sticky dough and sling it onto his face.

Violetta . . .

Granny Torrelli says, *Rosie, give Bailey a turn with that dough before you beat it to death.*

I shove the bowl at Bailey and go to the sink to wash my hands. I scrub them, rough, as if they are covered with tar. I feel Granny Torrelli's eyes on my back.

She says, *Did I ever tell you about Violetta?*

Nope, Bailey says. *Tell!*

Rosie? Granny Torrelli says. *You want to hear about Violetta?*

Sure, I say. Anything is better than hearing about nice, funny, curious Janine.

First I have to tell Bailey about Pardo, Granny Torrelli says. *Pardo was my buddy, my pal when I was growing up. We were like this, inseparable,* she says, squeezing her thumb and forefinger together, just as she did when she told me about Pardo. *Then one day, a girl comes to stay with her aunt, next door to Pardo. Her name is Violetta.*

The way Granny says her name, I hear a little ice queen in her voice.

Cool name, Bailey says, *Vee-oh-LET-a.*

Puh! Granny Torrelli says. *Well, I tell you, that name means little violet, but she was no little fragile violet, that Violetta. She swings into our village, all long curly hair and long legs and big mouth. Chia-chia-chia, chatterbox all day long.*

Bailey laughs. *Chia-chia-chia*, he says, echoing Granny Torrelli.

Granny Torrelli flicks her hand in the air, as if she is flicking away a fly. '*Oh, Pardo,*' *Violetta would say,* '*oh, Parrrrr-do, you are so strong, you are so handsome, you are so smart, please will you help me with this, and please will you help me with that?*'

I love it that Granny Torrelli has a little ice-queen tiger in her, too.

I tell you, that Violetta, she hypnotized Pardo! He was stumbling around as if he'd been kicked by a mule, all in a daze over Violetta.

I see Bailey smile, then stop midsmile. He is thinking. I wonder what about. I want to bore a little hole inside his head and see what he is thinking.

Granny Torrelli shifts her feet on the chair and

says, *I tell you, I am not too much liking this little Violetta chickie. I am not too much liking the way she is falling all over my buddy, my pal Pardo.*

Bailey turns his head toward me. I know he can't see my expression, but still I look down at my feet, stare at my shoes. I want to hear how Granny Torrelli handled the Violetta chickie, but there is a knock at the window behind me. I turn.

Uh-oh.

Janine . . .

Janine is standing outside, waving and smiling. I slink to the door, let her in, arrange my mouth into a smile, but it is so hard. I feel as if my face will crack into many pieces and fall onto the floor at her feet.

She hugs me. *Hey, Bailey!* she says, and rushes over to squeeze him to bits. *And who's this?* she says, smiling down on Granny Torrelli sitting in her chair.

This is Granny Torrelli, I say, and then add, dumbly, *She's mine.*

Granny Torrelli smiles at me, then at Janine. *You must be Janine.*

Oh! Janine says, tossing her frizzy cool black hair. *You've heard about me, then?*

Granny Torrelli says, *I heard a new, nice girl, name of Janine, moved into the neighborhood. I'm figuring that might be you.*

Janine beams at Granny Torrelli. *That's me!* she says brightly.

It is all I can do to keep my inside tiger from jumping out. I take a couple deep breaths, try to stay calm.

We're making pasta, I say.

Really? She draws the word out—*Reallllllly?*—as if making pasta is the most extraordinary thing she has ever heard of, ever in her life. *People really* make *pasta? That's so, so fascinating. Like, how do you do it?*

Granny Torrelli glances at me quickly, checking to see if my tiger is in rein, maybe. Granny explains to Janine about the flour and the eggs and the dough, but before she can finish, Janine interrupts her.

Oh, this is so extremely fascinating!

And I am thinking I will die if she stays to help us. I want to tie her up and throw her out the window.

Bailey is standing there smiling his smile at everyone. His hands are still in the dough bowl.

But I am rescued, at least from that one wretched thing. Janine says, *I would so love to stay and watch, but I can't.* She turns to Bailey. *I just went over to your house, Bailey, but your mom said you were here.*

Grrr. She didn't even come to see me, her new best friend?

Janine races on. *I just need to know, Bailey, what time tomorrow I can come for my first Braille lesson.*

Granny Torrelli heaves herself out of her chair and comes toward me, as if she is going to the sink. She gives me one quick look, a simple look but full of meaning. Her look is a warning to my tiger self, but it is something else, too, as if she is beaming me a little comfort.

And suddenly I am thinking, *Oh no, oh no, not tomorrow, please not tomorrow*, because I haven't yet reminded Bailey that tomorrow we are having the pasta party. Today we will make the pasta and the sauce, and tomorrow we will put it all together, me and Granny Torrelli and Bailey and Carmelita and my mom and pop. And I can't tell Bailey this now, because then Janine will want to come to the pasta party, too, and I don't want

Janine at our pasta party, even if she *is* my new best friend, who is not really my best friend at all.

But maybe Bailey knows about tomorrow, maybe Carmelita has told him, because he says to Janine, *I can't do it tomorrow, sorry. How about Monday after school?*

I am wanting to hug that Bailey boy for telling her not-tomorrow, but I am also wanting to slug him for Monday-after-school.

Janine does not miss a beat. *Oh, that's okay, Bailey. Monday is great! Perfect! You want to come to my house?*

Grrr.

Sure, Bailey says.

Perfect! she says, tossing the frizzy cool black hair.

'*Bye, Bailey* (squeezes his arm, pats his shoulder), '*bye, Granny Torrelli* (smiles her perfect white smile), '*bye, Rosie* (hugs my tiger self), '*bye, 'bye, 'bye!*

And she is gone, and we are left in the wake of all that smiling Janine girl.

Granny Torrelli is standing right next to me. As the door closes, she whispers in my ear one word: *Violetta.*

Haircut . . .

Terrible silence in the room for several long minutes, until Granny Torrelli examines the dough and says, *Okay, dough needs a little rest*, and she puts the bowl to one side. Bailey goes to the sink to wash his hands, and I flounder there in the middle of the kitchen, like a fish that has been thrown to shore.

Granny Torrelli sits back down and says, *So, you want to hear more about Vio-let-ta?*

Bailey and I answer quickly, *Yes!* as if we are both grateful for Granny filling up the silence in the room.

I am not too proud of what I am going to tell you, she says. *But I don't think you'll hold it against me.* She smiles at me. *So there is Violetta with the long beautiful hair, gushing over my Pardo, and there is Pardo like her little slave, helping her carry this and that, and I am turning into a monster, so mad at both of them.*

Granny Torrelli leans forward, lowers her voice as if what she is about to say is a secret. *So one day, I get that Violetta alone, and I ask her if she isn't hot with all that heavy hair hanging down her back. She says, 'Well, a little,' and I tell her that I bet she would feel so much better if she chopped all that long hair off, and I bet she would look really cute with short hair. This is not true, I do not think she would look really cute with short hair. I am a monster.*

Bailey dries his hands, sits at the table. *And?* he says. *And then what?*

I tell her I am a good haircutter (another lie), and I get the scissors and I convince Violetta to let me chop off her beautiful long hair.

No! I say. *Not really?*

Really, really, Granny Torrelli says, reaching up to finger her own hair which is tucked into a bun at the back of her head. *I chop, chop, chop, all that beautiful long hair falling on the ground, and in the middle of chopping, I get afraid, what am I doing? I slow down, be a little more careful, I even up the sides, take a little more off here, fiddle with it. The whole time Violetta is sitting there with her hands over her mouth, uttering little squeals as the hair falls away.*

Bailey is shaking his head. He can't believe my granny Torrelli would be a monster girl.

So I finish, Granny Torrelli says. *My hands are shaking. Violetta stands up, tosses her head, and I almost fall over dead when I take a good look at her.*

Was it that awful? I ask. I am already thinking of taking the scissors to Janine's head, snipping off all that cool frizzy black hair. *Did Violetta look really, really ugly?*

Granny Torrelli taps the table, one, two, three times. *No! She did not look ugly. She looked even more beautiful!*

Bailey laughs; I gasp.

But, but— I don't know what I want to say, too many things bubbling up in my throat. *And Pardo?* I finally say. *What did he think of Violetta's new short hair?*

Granny Torrelli says, *Puh! He thought she looked like a movie star!*

Granny Torrelli gets up, says, *Have to take a little*

pause, and off she goes to the bathroom, leaving me and Bailey alone in the too-quiet kitchen with the dough and thoughts of Janine and Violetta swirling in the air.

A Long Pause . . .

So quiet there in the kitchen, just me and Bailey while Granny Torrelli is taking her little pause. Then Bailey reaches across the table, finds my hand, and taps on it once, lightly. A little grin is on his face.

Rosie, are you jealous?

Puh! I say, just like Granny Torrelli. *Jealous? Me? Of what?*

Of Janine.

Janine? Jealous of Janine? Now why would I be jealous of Janine?

My mind is in a riot, thoughts racing around, crashing into one another. I *am* jealous, I know it, a million, zillion times jealous, but I can't stop myself.

Bailey taps my hand again. *I don't know why you would be jealous of Janine, unless you think that I would like her better than you, Rosie.*

Crash! Zing! Things flying around inside my head so fast. I am thinking, *Hurry, Granny, hurry, come back from your pause and rescue me before I say something utterly stupid.* But Granny is taking a long, long pause.

Finally I say, *Well, would you, Bailey? Would you like her better than me?*

I am shocked at my bold Rosie self. I want the

answer, but only if it is the right answer. If it is the wrong answer, I want Bailey to evaporate, and I want the whole world to vanish.

Bailey shrugs. *I don't think so*, he says.

That is his answer: *I don't think so*. My tiger is raging.

You don't think *so?* I say. *You don't* think *so?*

Bailey's mouth does a little scrunching thing. *Was that the wrong answer?* he says.

And then there is Granny Torrelli, back from her long pause, with his wrong answer hanging in the air, hanging heavily in the kitchen air.

Snakes . . .

Granny takes a look around, senses that maybe her pause should have been even longer, looks as if she is debating whether or not to leave the room again, but then she steps purposefully to the counter and lifts the bowl of dough.

Bene, she says, *I will do my little miracles and then we will make the snakes.*

Snakes? Bailey says.

Fun part, Granny says, *you'll see.* She sprinkles flour on one of the pastry boards, dumps the dough onto it, and then she kneads and pats and rolls the pasta with her hands, so graceful, so gentle, until the dough is gleaming and smooth. No more sticky patches. It looks beautiful. Then she shapes the dough into an oval and takes the big knife and slices off pieces, each one the size of a tiny lemon, and she places one lemon-size piece in front of each of us.

Flour your hands, she says, *like this.* She shows Bailey by letting him feel her own hands. *Now you make the snakes. Rosie, show Bailey.*

I glare at her. I am not wanting to show Bailey. Granny winks at me. I move over beside Bailey and take his hands and put them on the dough, with my hands on top of his. I show him how to roll with his fingers so the dough will get longer and thinner.

I stop being mad at Bailey while my hands are on his.

Oh, I get it, he says, and so I let go of his hands and stand back, watching as he swiftly rolls his dough into a perfect snake.

Inside, I am thinking good things and terrible things. I want to stay there watching Bailey forever. I want him never to leave. I do not want him ever to be with Janine. I hate Janine for coming to live in our neighborhood. I want the snakes to be real and slither off the table and under the door and over to Janine's and . . .

You going to help us, Rosie? Granny Torrelli says, jolting me out of my head, bringing me back to the kitchen and the dough.

We make all the snakes and then Granny tells me to chop them up, so I chop each snake into little inch-long pieces. I love the next part, when we make the little cavatelli.

Show Bailey, will you, Rosie? Granny Torrelli says,

and I am happy to put my hand on Bailey's again, and dip his fingers in the flour and then show him how to take one of the little pieces and roll it with his forefinger against his thumb, pressing in as he rolls, so the perfect shape is made: It looks like a little dough canoe.

Bene, bene, Granny Torrelli says, sitting across from us, watching me and Bailey, side by side, making the little dough canoes, the cavatelli. And for a time, it is peaceful in the kitchen, and I am outside myself, a calm place to be.

Sauce . . .

All the cavatelli are spread out on the floured board where they will dry. Granny Torrelli says, *Bene, bene, now it's sauce time,* and she has her nose in the refrigerator and is pulling out spareribs and ground beef and eggs and garlic and onion and tomatoes. From the cupboard she snatches salt and pepper and oregano and bay leaves and olive oil.

I am the director, she says. *Let's get this production moving!*

Granny dribbles olive oil in the big red pot, while

Bailey and I chop onions and garlic, and then we toss them in the pot, and what a smell in that kitchen, what a good, good smell!

Spareribs, Granny directs, and Bailey plunks the spareribs in the pot, where they sizzle.

Tomatoes, chopped, Granny says, and so we chop all the tomatoes while Granny opens the wee can of tomato paste, the thick, red, sticky paste that will go in the pot with the tomatoes.

As the spareribs are browning, I can't help it, I say, *So whatever happened to Violetta?*

Puh! Granny Torrelli says, settling herself on the chair and sniffing the good smells in the kitchen. *Here is the good thing that happened: Marco.*

Who's Marco? Bailey says.

Granny Torrelli grins a little-girl grin, full of

mischief. *Very cute boy, comes to stay with his grandmother, next door to me. Very smart boy, too, and molto charming.* Granny smiles at the ceiling as if Marco, the cute, smart, charming boy, is floating up there.

What does Marco have to do with Violetta? I ask.

Ah, Granny Torrelli says, *everything!* She waves her hand at the tomatoes. *Tomatoes in the pot,* she directs. We obey. *Stir. Tomato paste. Two cans of water. Stir.*

Now where were we? she says.

Marco, Bailey says.

Ah, si, si, Marco. So Marco comes to stay next door, and Marco finds me very enchanting. Really, that is the word he used: enchanting. It's different in Italian, but you understand what I'm saying? I am enchanting!

That Granny Torrelli makes me laugh. She makes Bailey laugh, too.

So Marco is at my house day and night, hanging around like a sick donkey, please will I come out and walk with him, please will I come for dinner, please, please, please.

Bailey's head is tilted upward again, his thinking pose.

Granny Torrelli flicks her fingers at the red pot, bubbling with all the good smells. *Bay leaf. Oregano, two pinches. Salt, three pinches. Pepper, lots.*

We toss it all in, stir.

Bailey says, *And what did Pardo think of Marco?*

Granny Torrelli claps her hands together. *Pardo hated him! Couldn't stand the sight of him!*

I am trying to picture it. There is a little play going on in my head. There is Pardo swooning over Violetta, and Granny Torrelli monster-cutting Violetta's hair, and Violetta ending up looking like a movie star, and then Marco moving in and swooning over my granny Torrelli, and Pardo hating Marco.

Bailey is nodding. *I get it*, he says. *The shoe is on the other foot now, right?*

Yes, how you say? Bull's-eye? You hit a bull's-eye, Bailey boy. At first, I do not get it, though, Granny Torrelli says. *At first, I think, 'Why is my life such a mess? Why did that Violetta have to come and steal Pardo's heart, and why did this Marco boy have to come and be such a nuisance?'*

And when she says that, I am thinking, *Why did that Janine girl have to come? Why, why, why?* And I am wanting to hear more, but Granny Torrelli says, *Stop. Meatballs.*

She pushes a bowl in front of Bailey, motions for me to get the ground meat and eggs and salt and onions, and soon we are mushing our hands in the meat mush, squishing it and squeezing it, and the garlic-onion-spareribs-bay-leaf-oregano-tomatoes are swirling in the big pot, and all the smells are wrapping around us, and I am dizzy with it, with the smells and the squished meat and the play going on in my head.

And I want to know everything, everything: What happened with Violetta and Pardo and Marco and Granny Torrelli, and what will happen with me and Bailey and Janine, and why is there no Marco who finds me enchanting?

The Yellow House...

What happens next is so strange that I wonder if it is the play in my head and not what is really happening.

I am standing there with my hands in the meat-ball mush, and Bailey's hands are right there in the bowl with mine, and I see a big truck coming slowly down the street, a moving van. It stops across the street, three doors down.

I don't believe it, I say.

What? Bailey says.

Granny's eyes follow mine. She stares out the window, smiles a little smile.

Moving van, I say. *Looks like it's stopping in front of that empty house almost across from yours, Bailey, the yellow one.*

Very funny, Bailey says.

No, really, Bailey, really, really. I take my hands out of the mush, go to the sink, stare out the window. A car pulls up behind the moving van. Two cars. In one: a woman and a little girl. In the other car: a man and two boys, maybe twins? Maybe my age, maybe a little older.

Bailey has joined me at the sink. *Tell me*, he says.

I describe what I see. I tell him about the moving van and the two cars, about the man and woman and little girl. I tell him—oh, how casually I tell him—about the two boys, maybe twins.

I don't believe it, he says. He is agitated, annoyed, hating that he can't see for himself if I am telling the truth.

I beam at Granny Torrelli. *Well, well, well*, I think. *Double Marco!*

Meatballs . . .

Bailey is back at the bowl, snatching bits of meat goo and rolling them into balls and dropping them straight into the red pot full of bubbling sauce.

Er, Bailey, Granny Torrelli says, *gently, gently. The little meatballs are feeling bruised.*

Hmph, Bailey mumbles. He slaps another meatball together, drops it in the pot. Hot red sauce splashes up, catching him on the wrist. He makes a face but says nothing.

Wanna go over and meet the new people? I ask Bailey.

Can't, he says. *I'm making meatballs. I thought you were helping.*

Granny swings her head from Bailey to me, a funny little expression on her face, and I can't quite read what it means. Then she says, *Gotta take a little pause*, and off she goes to the bathroom again, leaving me there with Bailey, the bruised meatballs, and the splashing sauce.

I put my hands in the bowl, make a meatball, gently, gently, and place it in Bailey's hand so he can put it in the pot. His hand floats there a minute, as if he is assessing the gift I've just given him. Then he plops it into the pot and says, *I thought you were going outside to introduce yourself to the new neighbors.*

I hear an ice king in his voice.

My first impulse is to say, *No, Bailey, I am staying with you here forever,* but something stops me, some little sly fox who has replaced my tiger.

I say nothing, which Bailey hates, I know it. Usually if I stop talking and he doesn't know why, he will put his hands on my face to read my expression, but his hands are sticky with meatballs, and so he does not put them on my face. I know it is mean of me to be quiet right now, but the sly fox has taken over, and I am no longer in control of my Rosie self.

Bailey reaches for the bowl, finds my hands in it, rests his hands on mine for the quickest second, then pushes my hands to one side and grabs some meatball mush.

I glance out the window. The new family is standing on the lawn talking to the truck drivers. One of the maybe-twin boys is dribbling a basketball.

Huh, I say to the air. *One of the new boys is dribbling a basketball.*

So? Bailey says.

My sly fox pounces. *I've always wanted to learn how to play basketball*, I say. And then, because my fox is really mean, I add, *Maybe they will teach me.*

Plop! I hear another meatball drop into the pot. *Plop, plop!* Two more.

Granny Torrelli reappears from her pause. She studies me, studies Bailey, frowns a little. *How's that sauce coming, Bailey? How are those meatballs?*

Couldn't be better, Bailey says, in an ice-king voice.

Not So Fast . . .

All the meatballs are in the pot, and Bailey is stirring. *Are we done?* he says.

Granny Torrelli says, *Let's see, cavatelli made and resting. Sauce and meatballs bubbling.*

Bailey takes off his apron. *Well*, he says, *I guess I'll be going.*

My fox disappears. I don't want Bailey to go. Maybe Granny Torrelli senses this, because she says, *Wait a minute, Bailey boy, don't you want to hear the end of Violetta-and-Pardo-and-Marco?*

Bailey hesitates. He doesn't look too happy.

Stay, Bailey, I say.

You two can wash up the bowls while I talk, Granny Torrelli says.

I wash, Bailey dries, Granny Torrelli talks.

So where were we? Ah, si, Marco hanging around like the sick donkey, me being enchanting. I am a little slow to figure it out, but pretty soon I realize that after my buddy, my pal Pardo has seen Marco hanging around my house, Pardo always comes over, pays a little attention, tells me Marco is stupido.

I am washing the meatball bowl, and already I am translating Pardo into Bailey, and I smile. I stare out the window at the maybe-twin boys, and I wonder if they will both find me enchanting, and if Bailey will tell me they are *stupido*.

Granny Torrelli shifts in her seat, props her feet. *Now Violetta starts noticing Marco. She is saying, 'Oh, Marco, you're so smart, you're so handsome, you're so strong, will you help me with this and will you help me with that?'*

I pass the meatball bowl to Bailey to dry, and I am thinking, *What? That Janine girl might set her sights on the maybe-twin boys, too? What a lot of nerve!*

And no kidding, just as I think this, I look out the window and there is that bouncy Janine girl, bouncing down the street, waving at the new neighbors. My tiger self wants to leap through the window, pounce. Part of me wants to dash out the door, beat her to it, and part of me wants to stay with Bailey and hear about Violetta and Marco and Pardo.

Bailey looks puzzled, I'm not sure why. He says to Granny Torrelli, *The web is getting very tangled.*

Si, si, Bailey, very true. Granny Torrelli's voice softens. *And then there was the Gattozzi baby.*

Who? I say, my head all jumbled, not able to concentrate as I see Janine bouncing, bouncing, bouncing along, and there she is right in front of the new neighbors. She is bending to cozy up with the little girl, smiling, tilting her head this way and that. I turn away, can't bear to watch.

Granny Torrelli has a sad look on her face. *The Gattozzis, they lived in our village, very nice family, with a new baby girl, most beautiful baby you ever saw in your life, but she got sick, very sick, and everyone was praying for her. I go to see the Gattozzis. I take them zuppa from my mother. They let me see the little baby, very flushed in her little basket, and I put my hand in and the baby grabs it and holds on. Her fingers are so hot and they hold very tight to my hand.*

I sit beside Granny Torrelli, take her hand. I am thinking, *Please don't tell me that baby died.*

It is quiet in the kitchen, with only the sounds of the bubbling sauce and the hum of the refrigerator.

I sit with the baby, Granny Torrelli says. *I sit all day long. She won't let go of my fingers. Her parents let me hold her, and still she is clinging to my fingers, and all the time I am sitting there with that little sick baby, I am not thinking of Violetta or Pardo or Marco. I am only thinking the baby must get better, the baby* must *get better.*

Bailey now joins us at the table. His expression is soft, gentle. His hand slips across the table and taps Granny Torrelli's wrist. She lets his hand stay there, while my fingers rest on her other hand.

It is so quiet and so sad there in the kitchen with our hands all on the table: Granny's wrinkly soft ones, and Bailey's strong ones and my normal Rosie ones.

The Baby . . .

Granny Torrelli sniffs. *Stir,* she says. I get up, stir the sauce, breathe in its spicy smell, and return to the table.

So, Granny Torrelli says, *the Gattozzi baby. I sit there all afternoon, holding the baby, until my sister comes to get me. The next morning I go back, with a bowl of pasta from my mother. The baby seems a little better, her mother says. I hold the baby, and her little hand clings to my fingers. And I start singing to her.* Granny Torrelli looks up at me and Bailey. *Maybe you think I am silly?*

We both shake our heads. No, we do not think she is silly. While she is talking, it's as if I am there in the village of my granny Torrelli, and I am holding the baby and I am singing to her.

I am singing the songs of my mother and my grandmother, Granny Torrelli says, *little lullabies I thought I'd forgotten. I sit there until my sister comes to get me again. Next morning, I go back, with more zuppa. Baby is gone! Parents gone! No one home! I am frantic! I sit on the steps and I sob like a little baby.*

And while I am listening to Granny Torrelli, I am frightened and I fear that I, too, might sob there in the kitchen with Bailey and Granny Torrelli. I look at Bailey. His head is down, and I want to lift it, to see his face.

Granny Torrelli says, *And while I am sitting there sobbing, I don't even hear the parents come up the walk. I jump when the mother taps my arm. And I think I am going to have a heart attack because there they are, holding the baby, and the baby is smiling, and they say, 'It's okay, she's better.' And they let me hold her, and that little Gattozzi baby holds my fingers so tight and I sing to her and I am so happy at that moment.*

A big relief sigh comes out of me, and Bailey lifts his head, and I see that he, too, is relieved.

And here is the thing, Bailey and Rosie, when I went home that day, I felt as if I was ten years older. I saw Violetta on her way to Pardo's and I saw Marco down the lane looking for me, and I can't explain it, but I felt as if my life was bigger now.

Bailey gets up, stirs the sauce.

And here is the ending, Granny Torrelli says, *or the beginning, depending on how you look at it: Soon Violetta went back to her regular home, and Marco went back to his, and it was me and Pardo again.* She shrugged. *Maybe it is not such an exciting story?*

I tap Granny Torrelli's hand. *It was just right.*

I walk Bailey to the door and remind him that tomorrow is the pasta party. My tiger and fox and ice queen must be asleep, because I hear myself say, *Maybe we should invite Janine?*

Bailey says, *Maybe you want to invite the new neighbors, too?*

I touch his arm. I say, *I don't care if the whole town comes, as long as you come, Bailey boy.*

He gives a little smile and feels his way down the steps and turns to wave.

I wave back, even though he can't see my wave. And I am thinking that I cannot control who is going to come and who is going to go, and who will stay my buddy, my pal, and who will find me enchanting, and oddly I feel relieved.

The Pasta Party . . .

It is Sunday, and Granny Torrelli and I set the table in the dining room, twelve places. We use the good china, which used to be Granny Torrelli's. It has tiny red roses on it and little green vines. Carmelita brought zinnias from her garden: red, yellow, orange, purple, and they are in a vase on the table.

Mom and Pop are upstairs getting dressed, and Bailey and Carmelita are in the kitchen heating up the sauce and the water for the cavatelli. Our house smells so good, looks so good.

And soon people are pouring in the door: first bouncy Janine with a box of chocolates and then Mr. and Mrs. Jefferson, the new neighbors, with their little girl, Lucille, and their two boys, who turn out not to be twins. They are Johnny (my age) and Jack (a year older). Lucille hands my mom a basket of fruit, and my mom bends down to thank her.

It is good that we are all crowded together in our little house, because if there were more room we would be more awkward with each other, I think.

Mom and Pop are chattering with Mr. and Mrs. Jefferson, Granny and Carmelita are chia-chia-chia-ing in the kitchen, Lucille is running from room to room, checking everything out.

Janine is bouncing from person to person, flashing her white teeth, and Bailey is talking with Johnny and Jack, and I am mostly listening and watching, enjoying that our house is filled up with people talking and laughing.

I carry the steaming bowl of cavatelli, covered with the beautiful red sauce, to the table, and Granny Torrelli brings the bowl of meatballs and spareribs, and Carmelita brings the extra sauce, and Bailey has the cheese, and Pop brings the salad, and Mom pours water in everyone's glass.

And Granny Torrelli bows her head and says grace, and at the end, she blesses her mama and papa and all her sisters and brothers and everyone at the table, and then she clinks her glass and says, *Here's to Rosie and Bailey, who made our delicious meal.*

And everyone raises a glass, and Bailey and I smile, and Granny Torrelli nods her head and says, *Tutto va bene.*

All is well.

Welcome to Pickleberry Street! Granny Torrelli says, and everyone laughs.

And I look around the table at all the people and then I look up at the ceiling and I think about Granny Torrelli's mama and papa and sisters and brothers and Pardo and my grandpa Torrelli, all up in heaven having their own pasta party, and my world seems a little bigger.

I look across the table again at Granny Torrelli, who is raising a forkful of cavatelli to her mouth. She pauses and says, again, but this time only to me: *Tutto va bene.*

And she is right.

SHARON CREECH is the author of the Newbery Medal winner WALK TWO MOONS and the Newbery Honor winner THE WANDERER. Her other novels include RUBY HOLLER, LOVE THAT DOG, BLOOMABILITY, ABSOLUTELY NORMAL CHAOS, CHASING REDBIRD, and PLEASING THE GHOST. She is also the author of two picture books, the *New York Times* best-seller A FINE, FINE SCHOOL and FISHING IN THE AIR. After spending eighteen years teaching and writing in Europe, Sharon Creech and her husband have returned to the United States to live.